NEW CHINATOWN

ALPINE ST.

Broadway

COLLEGE

ORD

SPRING STREET

STREET

STREET

CHINA CITY

NORTH MAIN STREET

RAILROADS, FACTORIES, WAREHOUSES

ELYSIAN PARK

LOS Angeles California

1940s

W

S —•— N

E

MACY STREET

Los Angeles River

*To the victims of wars past and present. And to my husband Michael
and daughters Crystal and Celena for their endless support.*
- I.S.

*To Jake Lee, my first watercolor instructor, and my five grandchildren—
Bryce, Austin, Grant, Ashley and Q.
I hope they grow up to appreciate all cultures as much as I do.*
- G.G. R.

MEI LING IN CHINA CITY

中國市的美玲

WRITTEN BY
ICY SMITH

ILLUSTRATED BY
GAYLE GARNER ROSKI

作者 Icy Smith 鄧瑞冰　　　　插圖 Gayle Garner Roski

Chinese translation by Zeng Fan 曾凡 翻譯

East West Discovery Press

Manhattan Beach, California

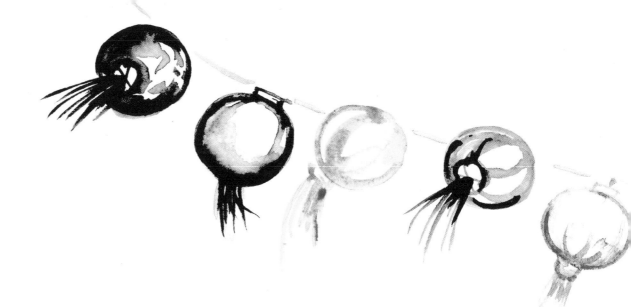

It has been three years since we moved to Los Angeles Chinatown from Oregon. Now we live in a small house on Alpine Street. My parents told me that the original Los Angeles Chinatown, called Old Chinatown, was demolished not long ago to build Union Station, the main train station in Los Angeles. In 1938, thousands of Chinese Americans were forced to relocate to other Chinese communities, and they were not treated very respectfully. Some moved to the area around City Market on 9th and San Pedro Streets, and some moved to the newly built China City and New Chinatown where we live. My family owns and runs a Chinese restaurant called Chung Dat Loo in China City where I waitress after school almost every day.

我們從俄勒岡州搬到洛杉磯的中國城已經三年了。現在我們住在愛盼街的一棟小房子裡。爸爸媽媽告訴我舊中國城，也就是最初的中國城早就被拆除了，在那裡建造了洛杉磯的主要火車站，聯合車站。在1938年，上千的美國華人得不到良好的尊重，被強制搬遷到其它華人社區。有些人移居到位於第九街和聖彼卓街的市場區附近，有些人則搬到新建造的中國市和我們現在住的新中國城。我們家在中國市經營一個叫昌達隆的中餐館，我幾乎每天放學後都要到餐館做服務員。

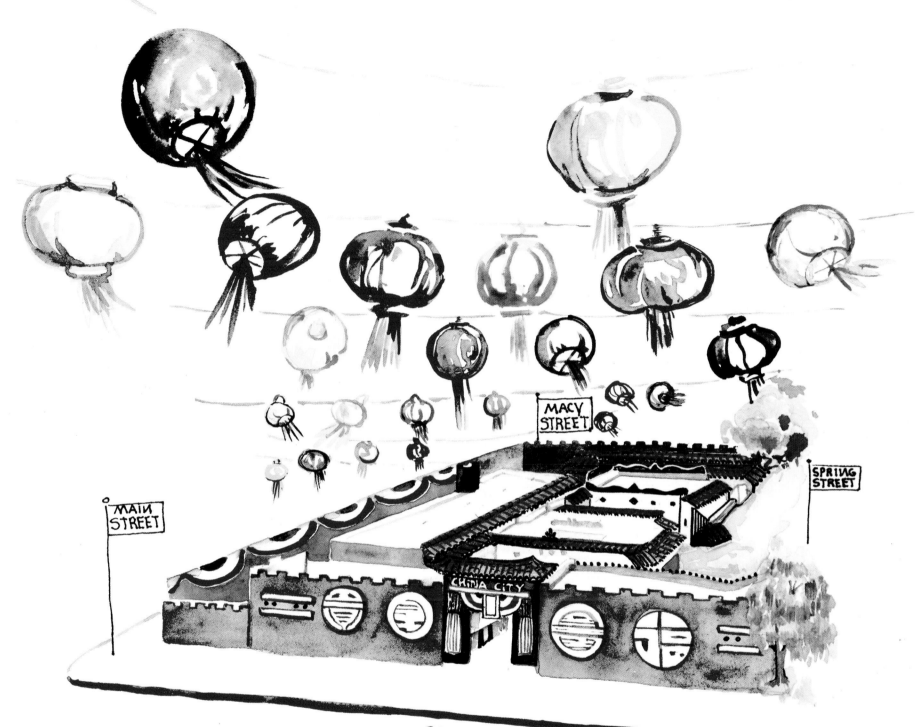

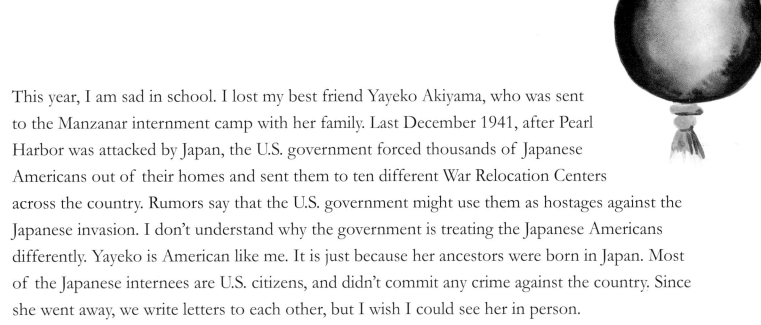

This year, I am sad in school. I lost my best friend Yayeko Akiyama, who was sent to the Manzanar internment camp with her family. Last December 1941, after Pearl Harbor was attacked by Japan, the U.S. government forced thousands of Japanese Americans out of their homes and sent them to ten different War Relocation Centers across the country. Rumors say that the U.S. government might use them as hostages against the Japanese invasion. I don't understand why the government is treating the Japanese Americans differently. Yayeko is American like me. It is just because her ancestors were born in Japan. Most of the Japanese internees are U.S. citizens, and didn't commit any crime against the country. Since she went away, we write letters to each other, but I wish I could see her in person.

今年我在學校很不開心。我失去了最好的朋友秋山八重子。她和她的家人被送到了在漫扎納(Manzanar) 的拘留營。在去年，1941年的12月日本襲擊了珍珠港之後，美國政府強迫所有的在美國的日本裔離開家園，搬進分佈在全國的十個不同的拘留營。謠傳美國政府要把他們作為人質來抵禦日本侵略。我不懂為什麼美國政府要對美國日本人另外對待。八重子像我一樣也是美國人，只是她的祖輩是生在日本。大多數被拘留的日本裔都是美國公民，他們沒有犯過任何反對美國的罪行。自從她離開後，我們一直相互通信，但是我希望看到她本人。

July 15, 1942

Dear Mei Ling,

Life is very difficult in this camp. I'm so bored. Manzanar is in a dry, windy desert with dust and sand everywhere. I wake up every morning with dust on my face. The Sierra Nevada Mountains create a high wall behind our camp, and I can see snow up there. The camp has a four-mile barbed wire fence around it with armed guards. There are guards in eight high watchtowers with their guns pointing inward toward us. We live in a crowded military-style barrack, eat in noisy mess hall with everyone else, and share the latrine and shower rooms. There is no privacy at all. I heard a few schools will be opened up here soon, but none have opened yet. I hope I don't get too far behind. But school will not be fun without you. I miss you and the good times we had. Did you make any new friends? Write to me soon.

Love,

Yayeko Akiyama

Manzanar, California

1942年7月15日

親愛的美玲：

在漫扎納的生活非常艱難。我覺得非常單調無聊。這是個沙漠地區，干燥多風，到處是塵土和沙礫。每天早晨醒來我的臉上都蒙著塵土。高聳的內華達塞亞山就像一道高牆豎立我們營房後面，我可以看見山上的積雪。拘留營週圍有四里長的鐵絲網和警衛人員巡邏，八個監視塔上的警衛持槍對著我們。我們住在擁擠的兵營一樣的屋子，在嘈雜的食堂吃飯，和其他拘留者共用廁所和淋浴。沒有一點私人的空間。聽說這兒很快就會有幾所學校，但是現在一個也沒有開始。希望我能夠跟上我的學業。 但是如果沒有你，學校生活也不會有樂趣。我真想念你和我們在一起的美好時光。你又交新朋友嗎？請盡快給我寫信。

愛你，
秋山八重子
於加州 漫扎納

Mom says, "The Moon Festival celebration is tomorrow and I want you to wear your silk dress. Only traditional Chinese clothes tomorrow, dear."

I go to my closet and pull out my long, red silk dress with yellow flowers hand embroidered on it. The last time I wore this was with Yayeko during the Chinese New Year festival last year. I try it on and it still fits me perfectly, but I am growing and this is likely the last time I will wear it. I remember last year walking down the street with my grandmother, who has bound feet, holding on to my arm. I am so happy that I was not born in China, where many girls' and women's feet were forced to fit into shoes about three inches long called lotus shoes. My grandmother told me that in the upper classes in China, foot binding usually began when a girl was three years old. A good marriage would be impossible to arrange if the girl had big ugly feet.

媽媽說 ：「明天過中秋節，我要你穿你的絲綢旗袍，明天只穿傳統中國服裝。」

我在衣櫥裡拿出我的紅色長旗袍，上面有手工刺繡的黃花。我上次穿它是去年過中國新年和八重子在一起的時候。我試了試，還很合身，可是我的身體還要長，可能這是我最後一次穿它了。我記得去年我的祖母牽著我的胳膊在街上走，她的腳是裹小的。我真高興我不是生在中國，在中國很多女孩和女人的腳被強迫裹小，要能穿進只有三寸長的稱為蓮鞋小鞋子。我的祖母告訴我在中國的上流社會中，女孩子們在三歲時就開始裹腳。如果一個姑娘長一雙大醜腳，那就找不到好人家出嫁。

Lotus Shoes

蓮鞋小鞋子

Today, we go to the restaurant early in preparation for the big crowd coming to China City. My dad is the main chef of our restaurant and is preparing the many ingredients for our most popular dishes such as Egg Foo Young, Cashew Nut Chicken, Chop Suey, and Fried Rice. They are Chinese American dishes, not really Chinese food, but it still tastes good to me.

"Mei Ling, go to Mr. Ling's gift shop to buy more lanterns. We need to get this place decorated properly," Pa yells to me, "and get a dozen more moon cakes, too."

今天我們都早早去餐館做準備，因為會有很多人來中國市。我爸爸是我們餐館的大廚，他做了很多的調料，都是用於那些最受歡迎的菜，比如芙蓉蛋，腰果雞，雜碎和炒飯。它們都是美國式中國菜，不是真正的中國菜，不過我認為它們味道很好。

「美玲，去林先生的禮品店多買些燈籠，這兒要裝飾的好看些，」爸爸高聲招呼我，「另外，再買十幾塊月餅。」

I walk up the staircase to Lotus Pool Road, passing the Golden Phoenix Restaurant, and stop by the Kuan Yin Temple to visit Johnny Yee. He is a good friend of mine and always has something entertaining to say. As I enter the temple, I immediately smell the fragrant incense and hear the soft chanting made by the Buddhists praying there. Johnny, who is seventeen, five years older than me, is wearing his long, black Chinese robe. This is not his normal outfit, but he says that's what the tourists like to see. He is selling a fortune-telling stick and incense to a passerby. "That'll be seven cents, please." The altar table is decorated with fruits, flowers, roast pig, moon cake, and tea.

我沿台階走上去，來到蓮花池路，經過鳳凰酒樓，在觀音廟停下看望易約翰尼。約翰尼是我的好朋友，他總是會說些逗人樂的話。一進廟，我立刻就聞到燒香的香氣，還聽到和尚們唸經時柔和的吟唱。約翰尼十七歲了，比我大五歲，他穿著黑色的中式長袍，這可不是他平時的打扮，他說他這樣的一身裝束正是旅客喜歡看到的。他正在向觀光客們叫賣運籤和貢香，「請買吧，七分錢一只。」祭臺上擺著的奉獻品有水果，花，烤豬，月餅和茶。

"Good morning, Johnny. Are you going to perform the lion dance in the parade today?" I ask.

"Yep, of course. Our troupe can't perform without me," Johnny smiles.

"How about you? You look nice today in your silk dress. Are you working for Mr. Gubbins today?"

Mr. Gubbins is an actors' agent for Asian American talent and has an office and film studio in China City. He specializes in hiring Chinese actors and extras for Hollywood movies. Many people from the neighborhood are recruited to act in movie productions. That is why China City is nicknamed the Chinese Movie Land.

"Not today. I am busy helping out at the restaurant, and in fact I have to get some lanterns right away. I'll see you later today in the parade," I reply.

「早晨好，約翰尼，你今天遊行的時候會表演舞獅子嗎？」我問。

「啊，當然了。缺了我他們表演不了。」約翰尼笑著回答。

「你好嗎？你今天穿著綢旗袍真漂亮。　今天你還要給古賓斯先生做事嗎？」

古賓斯先生是位發掘有才能的亞裔演員經紀人，他在中國市有間辦公室和一個電影拍攝場，專門替好萊塢電影僱用中國演員和臨時工。這個社區很多人都被僱用來拍電影，這就是人們把中國市戲稱為中國電影製片廠的原因。

「今天我不去，今天要在餐館幫忙，其實我現在正要去買燈籠。我們下午遊行時見。」我答道。

THE GOLDEN LANTERN

I run into the Golden Lantern Gift Shop and buy dozens of paper lanterns, then to the Che Kiang Importers for moon cakes. On my way back, I pass through the Court of Lotus Pools and see my friends Ruby, Frances, and Doris. They are holding American flags and have a tin box with the words United China Relief Fundraiser on it. They are collecting money for the people in China suffering because of the war.

"Hi, Mei Ling. Would you like to join us in our fundraising drive today? We're selling Chinese opera tickets and American flags. The top seller will win a $100 Chinese banquet gift certificate and a Chinese silk jacket," Ruby tells me. "We are selling the opera tickets and flags for $1 each. The money raised will help the women and children refugees in China."

"Oh. If you like, I can try to sell the tickets and flags at my parents' restaurant today," I reply.

"Great," says Ruby, as she hands over the flags and another tin box.

In my mind, I hope that the war will end soon so we can reconnect with our family in China, and our Japanese American friends here in the U.S. I hope the sick and displaced Chinese families in China will not suffer any more. I also want to see Yayeko and others come home.

我跑到金光燈籠禮品店買了幾打紙燈籠，然後又去浙江進口店買了月餅。在回來的路上，我穿過蓮花池的空場。在那兒，看見我的朋友魯比，弗朗西斯和多麗絲，她們手裡拿著美國國旗和錫盒，盒子上寫著「聯合中國救濟募捐」。他們在為中國的戰爭難民籌集捐款。

「嘿，美玲，你願意參加我們今天的捐款活動嗎？我們在賣中國戲票和美國國旗。籌款最多的人可以獲獎，獎品是一張一百美元的中餐禮卷和一件中國絲外套。」魯比告訴我。「一面國旗和一張劇票各賣一美元，所賣的錢將用來幫助在中國難民營的婦女和兒童。」

「好，如果你們同意，我可以在我父母的餐館賣戲票和國旗。」我回答。

「那好極了！」魯比說著，遞給我一些國旗和一個錫盒。

我心中希望戰爭儘早結束，那麼我就能夠和我在中國的親人和在美國的日本朋友恢復聯繫。我希望那些生病和離鄉背井的中國同胞不再受苦。我也想念八重子，我想看到她和其他人都能夠重返家園。

Back in my restaurant, I help Papa and Mom decorate the lanterns. Very soon, thousands of Southern Californians arrive in China City and gather at the Court of Four Seasons. The lion dance parade and firecrackers kick off the Moon Festival celebration. Some ride the traditional rickshaw for 25 cents. Others browse through the mysterious Chinese village with quaint bazaars, knick-knack stores, lotus pools, temples, and movie sets. Many support the war relief effort by buying American flags and tickets to see "Mulan" and "The Chinese Princess" operas. In China City, it is interesting to see the traditional Chinese operas performed in English only, because most of the audience do not speak Chinese.

Our restaurant is overflowing with customers coming from all over town. I take advantage of the opportunity to sell the tickets and flags to our customers. After the busy lunch time, Ruby comes in to my restaurant with a frown on her face.

回到餐館，我幫爸爸媽媽掛燈籠。不一會兒，成千的南加州的居民就來到中國市，聚集在四季池前的空場上。舞獅遊行和燃放鞭炮開啟了慶祝中秋節的活動。有些人花25美分乘坐人拉的傳統黃包車，其他人則在神秘的中國村遊逛，流連於那些出售精巧商品的店舖和各樣小裝飾雜品的貨攤，還有蓮花池，廟宇和電影棚。很多人都買了國旗和戲票，看中國劇「花木蘭」和「中國公主」的演出，以表示他們對救濟募捐的支持。在中國市，傳統的中國戲是用英文演唱的，因為大多數觀眾不講中文。這真是很有趣。

餐館十分擁擠，就餐的顧客來自四面八方。我借此乘機會賣掉很多國旗和戲票。最忙碌的午餐時間剛過，魯比皺著眉頭來到我們餐館。

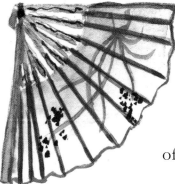

"How much did you raise so far?" Ruby asks. "Richard, who works at China Burger restaurant, seems to be winning the race. He has raised more than $70. I heard he offers the donors a free cup of coffee with each ticket or flag sold."

"Well, I've sold about $55. I'll think about some ways to sell more," I say. I think to myself, winning the fundraising drive is important to me. Besides helping the war victims, I want to save my prize for Yayeko when she returns home.

The weather is pretty hot today and that gives me an idea. "Hey, Ruby. I usually sell fresh-squeezed orange juice for 10 cents on the weekends. How about I give a free orange juice with each ticket or flag sold?"

"Great, that idea is perfect. I will help you squeeze the oranges," Ruby says with excitement.

Since the busy lunch time has passed, I have Mom's permission to make a fundraising booth just outside the restaurant, offering free cold orange juice.

「你籌集了多少錢？」魯比問。「在中國漢堡店工作的里查德看來要贏了。他籌集到70多美元。聽說他向每一位買戲票或買國旗的人提供一杯免費咖啡。」

我說：「我籌集到大約55美元，我來想想怎麼能夠多賣一些。」對我來說贏得籌款第一名非常重要，除了幫助戰爭難民外，我還想到我要把獎品保存好，等八重子回來後給她。

今天天氣非常熱，這給了我好主意。「喂，魯比，我通常在週末賣鮮榨橙汁，10美分一杯。我給每一位買戲票或買國旗的人提供一杯免費新鮮橙汁怎麼樣？」

「好極了，這個主意太好了。我來幫你榨橙子。」魯比激動的說。

由於午餐高峰期已經過去，在得到媽媽同意後，我在餐館外設了個募捐攤位，向捐助人提供免費鮮榨橙汁。

The colorful Moon Festival activities draw thousands of people. In no time, our orange juice stand attracts a long line of thirsty visitors. One familiar face comes to our stand. Ruby and I stare at her for a moment, realizing… it's Anna May Wong, who is a well-known actress!

"How much is the orange juice?" Anna May Wong asks.

"We are raising money for the children refugees in China. The opera tickets and flags are $1 each. Would you like to buy some?" I ask. Ruby just sits there, stunned.

Anna May Wong is impressed with our kind thoughts. She reaches for her Mandarin purse and flips open her wallet. She pulls out her checkbook and writes her donation to the United China Relief campaign.

"How many would you like?" I ask.

"Just one ticket and a flag, please."

After Anna May Wong leaves, Ruby and I look at the check with astonishment. It's for $300!

多姿多彩的中秋節慶祝活動吸引了上千的人，口渴的人們很快就在我的橙汁攤前排起了長隊。有一張熟悉的面孔出現在我們的攤前，魯比和我凝視她一刻，認出這就是黃霜柳，那個著名的演員啊！

「 橙汁多少錢一杯? 」黃霜柳問。

「我們在為中國難民營的孩子們募捐，戲票和國旗各都是一美元。您要買些嗎? 」我說。這時魯比只是楞楞的坐在哪兒。

黃霜柳被我們的善舉感動了，她把手放進她的中式手包，迅速打開錢包，拿出支票本，寫下她捐給聯合中國救災運動的數目。

「您要幾張戲票和幾面國旗? 」我問。

「請給我一樣一個。」

黃霜柳離開後，我和魯比驚訝的看著那張的支票，數額是三百美元！

August 7, 1942

Dear Yayeko,

Today in China City we celebrated the Moon Festival and raised funds for the United China Relief campaign. I think about refugees in war-torn countries. I think about you being trapped in that camp, too. I was the top seller of the fundraising drive. My prizes are a $100 Chinese banquet gift certificate and a Chinese silk jacket. I'm saving the gift certificate for you as food and clothing have become scarce these days. I miss you a lot. I hope the war will end soon. And I hope you will come home next Chinese New Year wearing your new Chinese silk jacket. Don't stop writing.

Love,

Mei Ling Lee
Los Angeles China City, California

1942年8月7日

親愛的八重子：

今天我們在中國市慶祝中秋節，並且為聯合中國救災運動募捐。我想念著受到戰爭創傷的國家的難民，也記掛著身陷拘留營的你。我贏得了籌款第一名。我得到的獎品是一張一百美元的中餐禮卷和一件中國絲外套。由於食品和衣服近來變得緊缺，我把獎品留給你。我非常想念你，希望戰爭早日結束，希望明年中國新年的時候你能夠穿上這件新的中國絲外套。不要不給我寫信。

愛你的

李美玲
於加州洛杉磯中國市

12-year-old Mei Ling Lee (today known as Marian Leng) in China City.
12歲的李美玲在中國市(現在叫 Marian Leng)

CHINESE NEW YEAR

1945

Author's Note

China City

In 1933, Old Chinatown was destroyed to make way for what was going to be Union Station, a major railroad terminal in downtown Los Angeles. Unfortunately, thousands of Chinese American residents were forced to relocate to crowded enclaves near the City Market on 9th and San Pedro Streets. The Chinese community and developers discussed many proposals and plans for a new Chinatown. Eventually, two separate settlements, new Chinatown and China City, were built in 1938.

China City was located adjacent to El Pueblo de Los Angeles, an area bounded by Spring Street on the west, Main Street on the east, Macy Street on the south and Ord Street on the north. China City was created primarily for tourism and was built with the support of Christine Sterling, a promoter of Olvera Street, and Harry Chandler, the publisher of *The Los Angeles Times*. Tourists could explore the "romance of the exotic Orient" by taking rickshaw rides for 25 cents and enjoy the traditional Chinese theater performed in English. China City depicted a mysterious Chinese village with curio shops, herb stores, temples and shrines, lotus pools, pagodas and popular restaurants. Displaced residents of the demolished Old Chinatown operated many businesses in China City.

The China City gateway on Ord Street with
Union Station in background.
Photo courtesy of Harry Quillen Collection.

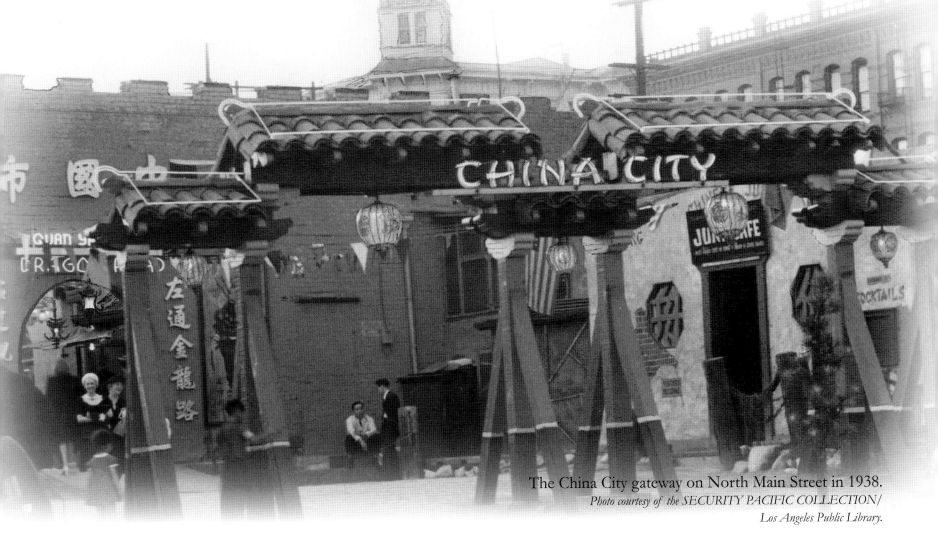

The China City gateway on North Main Street in 1938.
Photo courtesy of the SECURITY PACIFIC COLLECTION/
Los Angeles Public Library.

China City was also called Chinese Movie Land, with marketplace, rickshaws and replicas of life in China for the burgeoning Hollywood movie industry. Based on Pearl Buck's novel in 1940, the House of Wang set for the film *The Good Earth* was in China City. It was one of the first American movies that made any attempt to portray China and its people with sympathy. Chinese American workers in China City were called upon to act in many Hollywood motion pictures. Tom Gubbins was one of the Hollywood casting agents based in China City recruiting Chinese talent. Mei Ling Lee, Doris Chan, Frances Chan, Richard Sung Lee and Johnny Yee in this story had played various roles in many Hollywood films in the 1940s. Johnny Yee, who had several jobs in China City, thought it was funny that he had to learn Pidgin English in order to sound like he was Chinese. He, of course, was an all-American boy, although Chinese American. Anna May Wong was the first Chinese American actress to succeed in Hollywood, starring in many silent films in the 1920s and 1930s.

During the 1940s, China City was successful, with many thousands of visitors every year. It attracted a great deal of the city's attention. However, it was destroyed by a disastrous fire in 1949, and China City was never rebuilt. Today, a distinctive "Shanghai Street" neon sign on Ord Street is one of the few reminders of a once remarkable place. Although China City is demolished, its historic presence is fondly remembered by many Los Angeles elders.

Manzanar War Relocation Center

Japan attacked Pearl Harbor in Hawaii on December 7, 1941. Two months after this devastating event, President Franklin Roosevelt signed Executive Order 9066, which authorized the mass removal and incarceration of people of Japanese ancestry in the U.S., this due to so called "military necessity." Japanese Americans were believed to be potential spies for the Japanese government, and thought to pose a threat to national security. Without any proof of wrongdoing, close to 120,000 Japanese Americans were interned. About two-thirds of them were American citizens by birth. Manzanar, in the Owens Valley of California, was the first of ten War Relocation Centers across the U.S. during World War II. It had a population of approximately 11,000.

In 1983, the Commission on Wartime Relocation and Internment of Civilians, a congressional commission, finally declared that the internment was unjustified. The decision to incarcerate Japanese Americans was based on "race prejudice, war hysteria, and a failure of political leadership."

Today, Manzanar is designated a National Historic Site, and is visited by tens of thousands of people every year. The Manzanar legacy and the Japanese Americans who fought injustice to secure their constitutional rights should stand as a lesson to America to preserve human and civil rights of every person.

The real Yayeko Akiyama was actualy 15 years old when her family was uprooted and sent to the Poston War Relocation Center in 1942. Yayeko wrote many letters to her best friend Mei Ling Lee to recount her internment experience. However, Mei Ling did not receive any word from Yayeko after the war ended in 1945. Mei Ling, also known as Marian Leng today, is now in her eighties and hopes to see Yayeko again one day.

Entrance to the Manzanar War Relocation Center with the gatehouse in the background.
Photo courtesy of the Library of Congress, Ansel Adams, photographer, LC-DIG-ppprs-00226 DLC.

United China Relief

The Sino-Japanese War broke out in July 1937 in China. Japan launched a full-scale invasion of China, killing hundreds of thousands of Chinese civilians and soldiers. The war cut off Chinese Americans from their relatives in China. Horrifying reports of Japanese military atrocities in places like Nanking, the former capital city of China, galvanized Chinese American communities in the United States. To aid the suffering of war victims in China, United China Relief (UCR) held fundraising campaigns across the U.S. by organizing moon festivals, bazaars, fashion shows, and Chinese theatrical productions during World War II. The UCR fund was used to purchase food, medical and surgical supplies. By the end of World War II, the Chinese homeland was turned into a graveyard for an estimated 35 million innocents. The ethnic Chinese community in the U.S. raised a total of about $25 million for the war relief effort in China.

Lion dance at the Moon Festival to benefit the United China Relief.
Photo courtesy of the SECURITY PACIFIC COLLECTION/ Los Angeles Public Library.

作者註釋

中國市

在1933年，舊的中國城被拆除，為即將建造的位於洛杉磯市區的主要火車站,聯合車站讓出地方。不幸的是成千的美國華人被強制搬遷到位於第九街和聖彼卓街的市場區附近的擁擠居住區。社區華人和開發商討論了很多建造新中國城的計劃，最終，在1938年，建造了兩個分開的居住區，新中國城和中國市。

中國市緊鄰洛杉磯的艾爾普艾貝羅(El Pueblo de Los Angeles)，它西起士丙令街，東到緬街，南至梅西街，北達奧德街，主要是為招攬觀光客而建。中國市的建設得到奧維拉街 (Olvera Street)地產商克里斯庭.斯特林(Christine Sterling) 和洛杉磯時報的出版人哈里. 錢德勒(Harry Chandler)的支持。

遊客可以在中國市感受到東方浪漫的異國風采，花25美分乘坐黃包車，觀賞用英文表演的傳統中國戲劇。中國市的古董店，草藥舖，廟堂，蓮花池，塔樓和許多受人喜愛的餐館把神秘的中國村生活展現出來。許多的商業活動都是由從被拆除的舊中國城搬遷來的居民經營的。

在奧達街的中國市入口，背景是聯合車站。

Photo courtesy of Harry Quillen Collection.

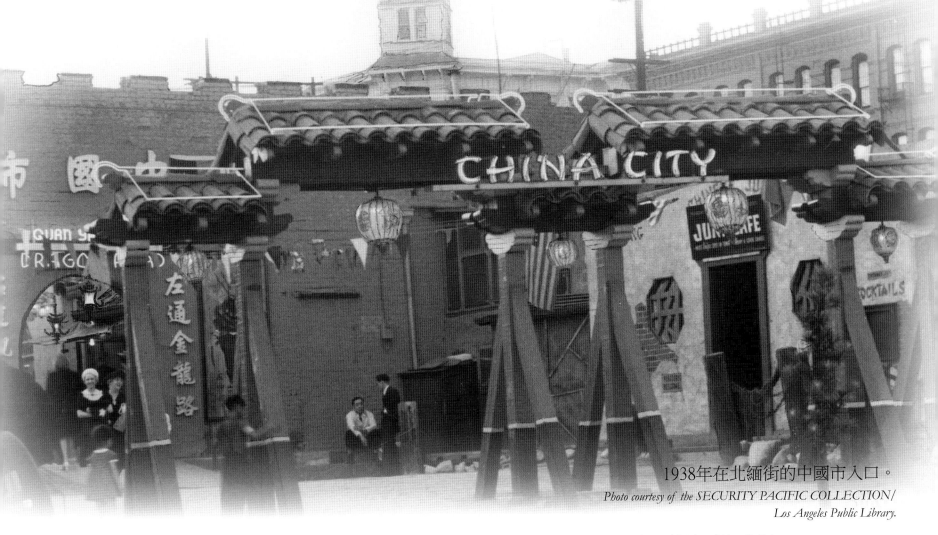

中國市也被稱為中國電影拍攝場，它的市集，黃包車，為迅速發展的好萊塢電影業提供了複製中國生活的場景。電影"美好的地球"（The Good Earth）是基於珀爾布克（Pearl Buck）1940年的小說，其中的佈景王氏房屋就是在中國市。該電影以同情的態度描述中國和中國人，是最早做這樣嘗試的幾部美國電影之一。中國市的美籍華工常常在好萊塢影片中扮演角色。湯姆古賓斯 (Tom Gubbins)就是好萊塢在中國市的經紀人之一，專門招募華裔表演人材。本故事中的人物李美玲(Mei Ling Lee)，陳多麗絲(Doris Chan)，陳弗朗西斯(Frances Chan)，宋李理查德 (Richard Sung Lee)和易約翰尼(Johnny Yee)在1940年代的許多好萊塢電影中扮演過不同的角色。在中國市打幾份工的易約翰尼說，為了演得像個中國人，他不得不學著說怪異混雜的英語，非常可笑。易約翰尼雖然是個華裔，但他是一個十足的美國男孩。黃霜柳就是第一個在好萊塢獲得成功的華裔女演員，她在1920至1930年代的很多無聲電影中出演。

中國市在1940年代很成功，每年都有成千的遊客來觀光，引起人們大量的關注。可是1949年的一場災難性大火把中國市燒毀，從此中國市就沒有再重建。今天，在奧德街獨特的霓虹燈招牌"上海街"是少數幾個存留物，令人記憶起那曾經著名的地方。中國市雖然被毀壞，但是它的歷史風貌卻仍舊留存很多洛杉磯的老人們美好的回憶中。

漫扎納(Manzanar)戰爭拘留營

日本在1941年12月7日襲擊了夏威夷的珍珠港。這個災難事件發生後兩個月,富蘭克林羅斯福(Franklin Roosevelt)總統簽署了9066號執行法令,授權把在美國的日本裔僑民大規模的遷移監禁,原因是所謂的軍事需要。日裔美人被認為有可能成為日本政府間諜,因而對美國的安全構成威脅。有約12萬在美國的日本裔被拘留,沒有任何證據說明他們做錯了任何事,其中三分之二的人是在美國出生的美國公民。漫扎納地處加州歐文斯谷(Owens Valley),是第二次世界大戰中跨越全美國的十個戰爭拘留營中的第一個。有大約一萬一千日裔被拘留在哪兒。

在1983年,美國國會的關於戰爭搬遷及拘留營問題委員會終於宣佈拘留營是不公正的。監禁在美國的日本裔的決定是在"種族歧視,戰爭狂亂狀和政治領導失誤"的背景下做出的。

現在漫扎納被定為國家歷史場所,每年都有幾千人去參觀。漫扎納的故事以及美籍日本人反對歧視保護自身憲法權力的鬥爭應該成為美國的保障人權和法權的一個教訓。

在1942年,秋山八重子15歲那年和全家被送到戰爭拘留營。八重子給最好的朋友李美玲寫了許多封信描述在拘留營的生活。然而1945年戰爭結束後美玲再沒有收到八重子的一個字。美玲(現名 Marian Leng)現在80多歲,仍然希望著有一天能夠再見到八重子。

漫扎納(Manzanar)戰爭拘留營的入口,
背景是入口的門房。

Photo courtesy of the Library of Congress,
Ansel Adams, photographer, LC-DIG-ppprs-00226 DLC.

聯合中國救濟運動

1937年7月爆發了中日戰爭，日本大規模侵略中國，殺戮了成千上萬的中國平民和士兵。戰爭中斷了美國華裔和他們在國內親友的聯繫。關於日本軍隊在華各地和前首都南京兇殘暴行的報告震驚激怒了在美國的華人社會，為支援在戰爭中受難的中國人民，聯合中國救濟運動在二戰期間在全美國發起了募捐，組織了中秋節，義賣，時裝展和製作表演中國戲劇等活動，募捐所得款項用於購買食品，藥品和手術器具。到第二次世界大戰結束時，中國大地變成了墳場，估計有三千五百萬無辜中國人死於戰爭。在美國的華裔社會總共籌集到二千五百萬美元支援救濟中國。

中秋節慶會舞獅表演為聯合中國救濟募捐。
Photo courtesy of the SECURITY PACIFIC COLLECTION/
Los Angeles Public Library.

The east gateway of China City on Main and Macy
Streets, surrounded by a "Great Wall."
位於緬街和梅西街的中國市東門入口。
Photo courtesy of Harry Quillen Collection.

Rickshaw driver Sinclair with Frances Chan in front of
Chung Dat Loo restaurant in China City.
在中國市的昌達隆餐館前拉黃包車的
Sinclair 和 Frances Chan。
*Photo courtesy of University of Southern California.,
on behalf of the USC Special Collections.*

Dragon dance in China City.
在中國市舞龍。
*Photo courtesy of "Seaver Center for Western History Research,
Los Angeles County Museum of Natural History.*

The Court of Four Seasons in China City with
Golden Phoenix Restaurant and China City Gift Shop
in the background.
中國市四季廣場，背景是鳳凰酒樓和中國市
禮品店。

Exterior view of the Chung Dat Loo restaurant owned
by Mei Ling Lee's parents in China City, 1940s.
李美玲父母40年代在中國市擁有的
昌達隆餐館的外觀。

Gilbert and Ronald Siu work as extras in the motion picture *The Good Earth*, based on Pearl Buck's novel, in 1940.

臨時演員 Gilbert 和 Ronald Siu 在電影 "美好的地球" 中表演。這部電影是根據 Pearl Buck 1940 年的小說製作。

Photo courtesy of SHADES OF L.A. ARCHIVES/ Los Angeles Public Library.

Anna May Wong was the first Chinese American woman to succeed in Hollywood, starring in silent films during the 1920s and 1930s.

黃霜柳就是第一個在好萊塢獲得成功的華裔女演員，她在1920至1930年代的很多無聲電影中出演。

Photo courtesy of Johnny Yee Collection.

Tom Gubbins, a Hollywood casting agent, recruits Chinese extras to act as Japanese soldiers during World War II. Luke Chan was one of hundreds of Chinese American actors in 1942.

好萊塢在中國市的經紀人 Tom Gubbins 在招募中國臨時演員扮演二戰中的日本士兵。 Luke Chan 就是在1942年的幾百位華裔臨時演員之一。

Photo courtesy of Johnny Yee Collection.

Pearl Jean Wong enjoys a rickshaw ride for
25 cents in China City.
Pearl Jean Wong 在中國市花
25 美分乘坐黃包車。

The House of Wang set from the film *The Good Earth*
with actor John Wesley Luck in China City.
電影"美好的地球"中的王氏房屋和演員
John Wesley Luck 在中國市。

Pearl Jean Wong at the Kuan Yin Temple in China City.
Pearl Jean Wong 在中國市的觀音廟。

Photo courtesy of University of Southern California., on behalf of the USC Special Collections.

Kuan Yin Temple in China City.
中國市的觀音廟。

Photo courtesy of Harry Quillen Collection.

16-year-old Johnny Yee at the Kuan Yin Temple in China City, 1941.
1941年16歲的 Johnny Yee在中國市的觀音廟。

Photo courtesy of Johnny Yee Collection.

Wong A. Loy and "Peanut Man" demonstrate martial arts in China City.
Wong A. Loy 和 "Peanut Man" 在中國市表演武術。

Photo courtesy of University of Southern California., on behalf of the USC Special Collections.

The Court of Lotus Pools in China City.
From left to right, holding umbrellas:
Dorothy Lam, Doris Chan and Ethel Wong.
在中國市蓮花池的空場，持傘從左右:
Dorothy Lam, Doris Chan 和 Ethel Wong。

Photo courtesy of University of Southern California., on behalf of the USC Special Collections.

Members of a Chinese band perform in China City. From left to right: "Peanut Man," Paul Fung, Mr. Tsin Nam Ling, Victor Wong, Wong Loy, and Ruby Ling.
中國樂隊成員在中國市表演，從左至右： "Peanut Man"，
Paul Fung, Mr. Tsin Nam Ling, Victor Wong, Wong Loy,
和 Ruby Ling 。

Photo courtesy of the SECURITY PACIFIC COLLECTION/Los Angeles Public Library.

Doris and Frances Chan play the butterfly harp
at the Moon Festival in China City, circa 1940.
1940年在中國市中秋節慶會上演奏楊琴的
Doris 和 Frances Chan 。
Photo courtesy of the SECURITY PACIFIC COLLECTION/
Los Angeles Public Library.

Chinese women's band in China City. From left to right:
Dorothy Siu, Pearl Jean Wong, unknown, Lillian Luck.
中國女子樂隊成員在中國市，從左至右：Dorothy
Siu, Pearl Jean Wong，無名氏，Lillian Luck 。
Photo courtesy of "Seaver Center for Western History Research,
Los Angeles County Museum of Natural History.

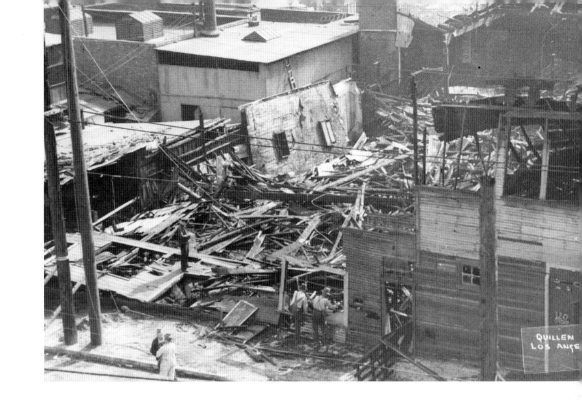

China City was destroyed by fire in early 1939. Some of the businesses had to relocate to New Chinatown. However, China City was soon rebuilt.
中國市在1938年受到第一次大火摧毀，有些商店被迫搬遷到新中國城，但是中國市很快就重建了。
Photo courtesy of the SECURITY PACIFIC COLLECTION/Los Angeles Public Library.

Theatrical actors wearing traditional opera costumes on stage in China City.
在中國市戲劇演員在舞台上穿著傳統的戲裝。
Photo courtesy of the SECURITY PACIFIC COLLECTION/
Los Angeles Public Library.

Text copyright © 2008 by Icy Smith
Illustrations copyright © 2008 by Gayle Garner Roski

Published by:
East West Discovery Press
P.O. Box 3585, Manhattan Beach, CA 90266
Phone: 310-545-3730, Fax: 310-545-3731
Website: www.eastwestdiscovery.com

Written by Icy Smith
Illustrated by Gayle Garner Roski
Edited by Marcie Rouman
Design and production by Luzelena Rodriguez
Production management by Icy Smith

ISBN-13: 978-0-9799339-5-0 Hardcover
Library of Congress Control Number: 2007937882
First Bilingual English and Chinese Edition 2008
Second printing 2010
Printed in China
Published in the United States of America

Mei Ling in China City is available in English and two bilingual editions including
English with Chinese and Japanese.